THE IMMIGRATION
LAWYER

Asylum

Shah Peerally

Dedicated to my wife, Feilah, my son, Abel, my daughter, Sarah, my parents and brothers, and everyone who fights for civil and human rights!

Rightful liberty is unobstructed action according to our will within limits drawn around us by the equal rights of others. I do not add 'within the limits of the law' because law is often but the tyrant's will, and always so when it violates the rights of the individual.

—Thomas Jefferson

In the aftermath of the September 11, 2001 terrorist attacks, hundreds of individuals were arrested without being charged. While most of those arrested were never convicted of terrorism, their greatest vulnerability had been targeted—their status as immigrants, individuals with the vulnerable tag of being outsiders. The defunct Immigration and Naturalization Services were absorbed into one unit named the Department of Homeland Security. Under the Patriot Act and the Real ID Act, the immigrant community was forced to live in fear. Many were deported or disappeared. In this time of darkness, emerged a group of civil rights lawyers, guerrilla lawyers. These lawyers believed in the United States Constitution and were determined to fight for justice. Their faith and allegiance were often questioned, yet none of them gave up. Among this group was a less applauded group, which consisted of those faced with the actual challenge, the implementation of the immigration law and new challenges namely being considered guilty until proven innocent. These were the immigration lawyers. They fought for equal access to justice, which should never be decided by skin color, religion, or nationality. This is the story of some of those lawyers and their fight that helped others gain the courage to raise their voices against injustice.

PROLOGUE

In Iraq

The year is 2002. Somewhere in the Middle East, in a cold dungeon, sits a man named Ahmad. There is no light. The room is so cold the man's presence can barely be seen or felt. The room is dirty and not furnished with anything—not even hope. From afar, one can see that the man is tied up and that he carries huge weights attached to his neck, which his body does not have the strength to bear. He appears miserable as he coughs and sweats. Peace is far, far away.

He bows to his death and awaits the torture that he knows will surely come again. His days and nights—he knows not which are which—are full of a peculiar kind of questioning that he does not understand. It is as if his torturers want him to say something that he has no idea about. He is asked over and over again whether

ix

he belongs to the CIA or whether he has any connection to the Islamic Brotherhood. He weeps, screams, and reads the Quran in between the torture sessions. There is neither food nor water—not even when they promise it—until he says what they want to hear. At times, the pain is too much for him to bear, and he lapses into silence.

In his dream-like stupor of pain and misery, he remembers the girl. The pain has made his head fuzzy, but he remembers her still. The torturer had brought her and dragged her in. They knew very well what effect this would have on him. They had looked at him and laughed while they ripped her clothes. "Not her!" he had screamed. Everything else was a blank after that. Ahmad had passed out: perhaps dying would have been more pleasant.

CHAPTER 1

SARAH, THE IMMIGRATION LAWYER, FINDS HER MISSION

The SPLG Legal Team

It is a normal working day for Shah, an immigration lawyer with SPLG, an immigration law firm in California, when a sudden knock at the door reveals the long-lost face of a friend: Sarah. Shah and Sarah have been friends for a long time, and they greet each other with warmth. Born in Fiji, Sarah is a well-known corporate lawyer in her own right. As Sarah begins to talk with Shah, she confides that despite having a good career in corporate law and being happy on the home front, she craves doing something more that will both satisfy her soul and give her an opportunity to be associated with people in their hour of need. Her role as a corporate lawyer is not gratifying enough for Sarah. She is married to a Caucasian Muslim from Bosnia, who is a firm believer in the Constitution of the United States. She thinks she can only be satisfied in her career if she can protect innocent people, in trouble.

Shah's Office at SPLG

As a successful lawyer with zeal for working with the community, Shah understands this perfectly well. His own staunch and constant support of the United States Constitution and his decision to work with the government instead of against it has earned him the appreciation and respect of friends, well-wishers, and colleagues. Sarah has offered her services with the will and dedication that Shah has always admired in his team. However, he now wonders whether his firm can afford Sarah, who is a well-established lawyer herself. But like all good things, Sarah too has perhaps come to the SPLG office with a higher purpose in life. Both of them soon decide to work together for the benefit of the immigrant community. Sarah somehow reminds Shah of his beginning as an immigration lawyer. Shah is impressed with Sarah's willingness to help, and he is delighted to have her on his team because he knows how important a good lawyer is to a case, especially for insecure immigrants who look up to their lawyers with a great sense of security.

Sarah Mustafagic, Attorney at Law

Meanwhile, a drama is unfolding at the San Francisco International Airport. A man walks up to an immigration counter. He is weak and appears nervous. The man is Ahmad. He is confident, though, because he has a valid B1/B2 visitor visa. The B1/B2 visa is commonly used when someone wants to visit as a tourist or try to enter the United States for a casual prospect of business. While handling his rather heavy luggage, he hands over his passport and visa to the officer who is in charge and waits for his turn. Perhaps, like many other visitors to the United States, Ahmad is eager to be visiting the land of dreams and opportunities. However, Ahmad could not have imagined even in his darkest moments what is about to unfold. Like any other visitor, at the immigration counter, Ahmad is asked why he is visiting the US and how long he intends to stay. Ahmad informs the immigration officer calmly that he is on a personal visit to see his family and that this is his third visit to the US in the past three years. However, something in the officer's tone and direction of questioning unsettles Ahmad, and he speaks with some difficulty. Then, as the officer begins asking questions that are clearly a departure from the routine, Ahmad senses trouble. The officer asks him why he keeps coming to the US, why he is arriving from Iraq, whether he has overstayed, what kinds of projects he works on, and so forth—certainly not questions one would expect an average tourist to be asked in the normal course of an interview. True to Ahmad's suspicion, the tone of the officer quickly morphs from courteous and official to a practically rude bark. The officer asks Ahmad to step into a secondary inspection room, where an intensive interrogation begins.

The immigration supervisor, an officer from the Customs Border Patrol, a branch of the Department of Homeland Security, conducts the interrogation. The immigration supervisor asks Ahmad about his mother, his origins, and his previous arrest in Iraq. But in spite of Ahmad's insistence that his arrest was purely political and that the purpose of his visit to the US is simply to see his family, the officers are unsympathetic. He is repeatedly asked about a notebook found in his bag, which has the names of various chemicals and US sites. Ahmad informs them that he is a chemical engineer, but to his dismay and utter shock, he finds himself being placed in custody by Immigration and Customs Enforcement officials. He is told that holding a legitimate US visa does not guarantee him entry into the United States, and he could, quite conceivably, be sent back. Ahmad is now scared out of his wits, adamant that he cannot go back, as he believes he will be tortured again if he returns. He decides to seek political asylum and informs the officers that he wants the protection of the United States. In a stunning turn of events, however, Ahmad is soon handcuffed, put in an orange jumpsuit, and escorted to a maximum security facility. Desperate but strong, Ahmad's only solace is now his faith and his prayers.

Ahmad at the San Francisco Airport

Here, the story begins to get interesting, and what unfolds before one's eyes is one of the most appalling examples of abuses of discretion by the authorities.

It is a peaceful day when the SPLG law office receives a frantic call from Muhammad. Once he has identified himself as Ahmad's brother, Muhammad is directed to Sarah, who listens to him patiently. Muhammad is extremely anxious about his brother, but Sarah calms him down and then asks him to narrate once again the string of events leading up to Ahmad's arrest, while she makes mental notes of the mysterious circumstances. She then reassures Muhammad and asks him to give the law firm the authorization for representation, and she immediately begins tracking down where Ahmad is being held. Several calls later, she discovers that Ahmad is being held at the maximum security prison in San Jose, California. For Sarah, her work for a given client begins the moment the clarion call comes in, and despite the fact that she has not been legally hired at the firm yet, she begins her job, conducting background checks on the prison facility where Ahmad has been incarcerated and will soon be relocated for custody. The law firm assures Muhammad, who is a dentist and a US citizen, that they will do their best to help Ahmad. Muhammad, nevertheless, feels helpless at this stage, unable to do anything, even as a US citizen.

Unlike many other immigration lawyers, helping a client who is in trouble goes well beyond Sarah's job duties. She is driven, to say the least, and Ahmad's release is now at the center of her thoughts. Driving quickly, Sarah soon finds herself in the confines of the maximum security prison in San Jose. A cold and dreary dungeon, it's a scary place for anyone, let alone a woman. Here, in something resembling a scene from one of those disturbing prison movies, Sarah is guided down narrow, dingy corridors by a voice coming through speakers. She rides prison elevators and passes through dark chambers where ribald, lecherous prisoners make lewd remarks and gestures at her. Unfazed, Sarah soldiers on, ultimately finding herself in a small cell. Here she meets Ahmad, who in spite of his predicament appears surprisingly calm.

Sarah Visiting Ahmad in Custody

At first, to break the ice, Sarah makes small talk by inquiring about Ahmad's family and his past. Then she gets to the crux of the matter, asking him about the interrogation process that he has been through and the reasons why he has gone through them. Suddenly, as they are talking, commotion erupts around them, and all of the shutters begin slamming down. To her disbelief, Sarah realizes that she, too, has been locked in. But before she can panic, a prison officer informs her that he is locking her in, along with all others, as they have a lockdown situation at the facility. Sarah, although an experienced lawyer, is not really familiar with the prison system. She is actually scared. Sarah wonders whether all of this is really happening to her or whether she is witnessing a sequence from a horror film. Just then, in a bizarre series of events, she sees a half-naked man run around and duck into the room she is in. Even though the security officials show up immediately, it is terrifying to find herself in this situation, despite Ahmad coming to her rescue and pushing her behind him. To everyone's relief, however, the uproar is quickly quelled, even though the lockdown continues for another hour. Sarah eventually leaves the prison with poise and with her sanity intact, though she is a bit shaken at the turn of events. The experience has been one of the most frightening of her life. Still, as a professional, she takes it in stride. In fact, she considers it a learning process. Apart from being briefly terrified, she has learned more about Ahmad. She now knows that not only is he someone who has endured torture, but that he is a man who can come to the aid of a woman when necessary—a very small revelation, perhaps, but something that gives a clear indication of the nature of the person she is dealing with. She is now more determined than ever to secure Ahmad's release.

Sarah Walking Down the Corridor of the Maximum Security Facility

For Sarah, the case is now no longer just a case. People both at her work and her home are concerned about her well-being. In the past, she has tended to go completely out of her way, becoming deeply and personally involved in helping her clients. She seeks Shah's advice in the case, as she is about to begin preliminary investigations and believes that taking him into confidence and soliciting his advice will give her some valuable input. Sarah tells Shah about the necessity of getting Ahmad released immediately, as his family does not have the financial wherewithal for a protracted legal case. On hearing this, Shah advises her to use the ankle bracelet program, in which the prisoner can be released from prison and placed under house arrest, where he is forced to wear anklets. He believes that Ahmad would be far more comfortable in a house, even with restrictive anklets, than in a prison cell.

Sarah Conferring with Shah

Sarah arranges for Ahmad to go through what is known as the credible fear interview at the ICE (Immigration and Custom Enforcement) office. In such an interview, the applicant is required to prove to the interviewer that he actually has a legitimate fear of going back to his previous circumstances. Ahmad passes the credible fear interview, and the interviewing officer recommends that he be released to wear an ankle bracelet. Family and life are strange, and sometimes even the most trivial of things are a cause for celebration: on the day Ahmad is released, his entire family is there to receive him. It is a happy occasion, and the family thanks Sarah for her part in bringing him home, where he is far better off than a prison cell. Sarah, however, knows that the battle has just begun, even though she relishes the familiar warm feeling that comes with helping someone in need.

One day, amid the regular hustle and bustle of the law office, Sarah receives a call from an unknown number. A long-forgotten woman's voice is at the other end of it. Sarah is puzzled as she tries to guess who the caller is. Slowly, the memory cloud clears, and she lets out a small, joyous shriek as she recognizes the voice of her long-time friend, Anisha Adath. Sarah has not seen Anisha since their law-school days. The excited ladies exchange fond memories and decide to meet for lunch. Between eating good Indian food, excitedly chattering, and catching up with an old friend, Sarah discovers that her friend now works with the FBI. With her ancestry in Lahore, Pakistan, Anisha is a practicing Muslim and a proud American. The FBI recruited her at the end of law school, right after she passed the bar exam with top grades. She sees her stint at the FBI as an opportunity to prove that religion is unrelated to being a citizen of the United States.

Sarah Talking to Anisha on the Phone

Sarah congratulates her friend on her job and her honest attempts to serve her country. As is always the case when two professionals in somewhat similar lines of work meet, they inevitably end up discussing their work. But still, Sarah is surprised when Anisha mentions Ahmad's case as the one she is working on. It then dawns on Sarah that the call and subsequent meeting with Anisha might actually indicate an ulterior motive for the lunch, rather than just two friends rediscovering each other. Sarah becomes upset that two long-lost friends cannot meet without work dictating their intentions. She is suspicious of her friend, especially when Anisha begins to discuss the case. She feels that her trust has been betrayed and that her friend has come not to see her but to talk about her client's case. She firmly believes that friendship should never be mixed with one's profession, and if one has to talk about work, it is courteous to be forewarned. Here, she would have preferred it if Anisha had told her beforehand that she was working on Ahmad's case and needed to talk to Sarah about it, instead of claiming that she was meeting a long-lost friend and that it was a coincidence that they were both working on the same case. Abruptly, Sarah flares up and asks Anisha the real reason that she wanted to meet her. Sarah asks her whether she thinks that working on this particular case means that she is biased toward her own community. Anisha protests that she is only doing her job and protecting her country. Sarah, in turn, reminds Anisha that they have both taken the same oath to defend and protect their country, but she cannot understand why people are mistreating and targeting innocent victims in her community. In spite of Anisha's insistence that they both belong to the same community, Sarah is furious with Anisha, stating that innocent people are being picked up at random, jailed on the slightest pretext, denied the right to proper counsel, and often branded as criminals without ever being tried and found guilty.

From a neutral perspective, both women are ostensibly arguing for the same cause, yet their methods are wildly different. When Anisha makes it clear that she is only interested in knowing whether Sarah's client is a terrorist, Sarah is outraged, and asks why the government is targeting innocent people who might be Muslim but are far removed from any terrorist activity. She adds that it is unfair to lump everyone into the same category simply because they belong to the same religion, and it can only instill anger and a sense of injustice among the innocent. Sarah is echoing the voices of many thousands of people who have been treated badly in the aftermath of the 9/11 tragedies. Sarah is also a personification of the ultimate free nation, the United States, which stands as a country that has been built over the years by people from different parts of the world. Each community has uniquely contributed to the strength of the nation, and until this time they all earned their respect and proud status as Americans, above all else.

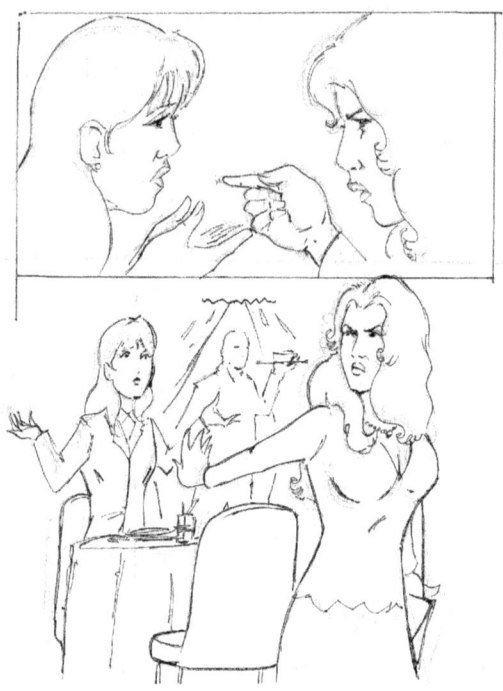

Sarah Upset at Anisha

Anisha, on the other hand, is just as adamant that people who have killed in the name of Islam have caused the innocent to suffer, they are looked upon with equal suspicion. It is indeed ironic, that the women belong to the same community, but they are fighting for a good cause from diametrically opposite points. While Sarah is striving to save the life of an innocent person who she believes to be wrongly accused, Anisha is trying to find out whether there are some people who in the name of Islam are tarnishing the name of the religion.

Each of the women know that the other might be right, but what has hurt Sarah is that Anisha has likely tried to exploit their friendship to extract information from her about her client. She had come to meet her friend in good faith for the first time in ten years, but now she feels cheated. As she walks out of the restaurant, wishing that she hadn't spoiled her afternoon, she is distraught and visibly angry at the thought of people exploiting others for their gain. Like her friend, Anisha too is disturbed. She realizes that she may have handled the situation rather insensitively, but she has faith in the system, and she thinks that she has convinced Sarah that all that she wants to do is prevent people from getting hurt, no matter which religion they belong to.

In the course of our lives, not every situation remains the same, and sometimes, in spite of our wariness and best efforts, we find ourselves wrapped in circumstances that are far different from what we might have imagined. This is the case with Anisha, who finds herself in a similar situation when her dedication to her job is questioned. She finds her boss insisting that she interview people at the local mosque, yet when she explains that she already has done so and that she is convinced that they don't know anything. Her boss presses her to talk to them again to find out about sleeper cells existing in the community. Anisha is irritated, to say the least, and she advises her boss that being from the same community she understands them much better than anyone else. As such, she can vouch for them and unequivocally state that there are no sleeper cells there. Her work and integrity are being undermined and has led Anisha's idealism to be rocked back on its heels. She truly believes that she is working to protect American citizens, irrespective of religion, and to that end she has betrayed her own community. But Anisha is no fool. She understands that her boss is asking her to conduct a witch hunt.

Anisha Arguing with Her Boss

For perhaps the first time in her career, Anisha voices her opinion. She regrets revealing that she grew up in the same community as the people she is investigating—the one that her boss associates with terrorism. However, she failed to take into account the fact that people from the same community do not always think alike. At this juncture, Anisha feels utterly drained and exhausted. Despite all of her hard work in the bureau, her courage, her search for the truth, and her allegiance is being questioned. Perhaps for the first time, Anisha understands the sense of pain that Ahmad and Sarah feel when they speak of innocent people being victimized in the name of security. Anisha is livid at her boss for questioning her allegiance, and she scolds her boss for his behavior. She literally grabs him by the collar and reminds him of all the honorable medals that the very same bureau has bestowed upon her. During the heated argument, in a fit of anger and frustration, when her boss threatens to suspend her, Anisha resigns from her job. For her, it has now become a matter of integrity. This is more important than earning money and retaining a job. In this one act, Anisha shows the strength of her character and her convictions about distinguishing right from wrong, no matter what the consequences.

Women such as Sarah and Anisha are perhaps the best professionals and the best friends because they are not only good at what they do, but they are passionate about what they do as well. They do not compromise their convictions and passions, no matter how difficult the journey ahead is. Anisha quit her job to prove her point and retain her integrity, and Sarah also knows full well the gravity of what she has taken on. It is not going to be an easy case; it will be full of hurdles, tense moments, and periods of fear. However, Sarah's zeal for what she believes in, gives her courage. She will need this more often than she has bargained for.

One evening, Sarah makes her way out of her office and into the parking lot at the SPLG headquarters. The place is almost deserted, but Sarah is too tired to notice. She has been working late, and she feels exhausted. Her body appears to have switched into auto-mode as she walks toward her car. Still, like all women, Sarah is blessed with good instincts, and she suddenly senses that she is being followed by three men. However, it is to late for her to react. One of her followers is already too close. Sarah panics and screams, even as a man grabs her by the hair and faces her toward the wall, muttering obscenities and trying to tear her clothes off and bang her face against the wall. They sneer at her, calling her a terrorist lover and roughing her up. As Sarah tries to escape and scream for help, a voice from behind yells: "FBI. Drop your weapons."

Sarah Attacked While Going Home

Sarah could almost cry with joy when she sees Anisha appear, out of nowhere, holding the gun. She is there to save her. Anisha is at this point more of an FBI agent than a friend. She points the gun at the hooligans and says in a dead, cold voice that the next shot will be aimed at them if they do not leave Sarah alone. While she is trying to check on Sarah, the three men have a chance to escape. Something about her face and steely voice seems to have scared the three guys, as they make a hurried exit, leaving behind a stunned and shocked Sarah, who is crying and throwing up. Anisha comforts Sarah and huddles her back into the safety of her car. Still crying and in shock, when Sarah finally arrives home, she is greeted by her worried husband. Like any loving husband, Adil is horrified at what has occurred. They did not know that the price of standing up for the truth would actually affect them in such a manner. Between comforting Sarah and trying to soothe her, Adil is adamant that he will have a talk with Shah and ask him to take Sarah off the case. As Sarah tries to tell him that she will be able to handle it, they hear visitors at the door. They are now even more scared, and Sarah's husband tells her and their children to go inside. However at that very moment, Anisha calls out from behind the door. Hearing her voice, Sarah relaxes. Sarah's husband is not too welcoming of Anisha at this hour. After thanking her for saving Sarah's life, he asks her politely but curtly if it is absolutely necessary to talk right then. Anisha has, however, come with two reporters, Abel and Mary, who work for an organization that fights against racism, and they say they want to interview Sarah.

Sarah, Abel, Anisha, and Mary

It is perhaps not a coincidence that Abel is a liberal who borders on the radical belief in equality, freedom, and human rights. He has devoted his life to protecting the rights of the weak. With a degree in political science and a major in communication, his work at one of America's biggest radio stations has been praised, along with that of his co-host, Mary. Mary is a free-spirited, street-smart journalist who is ready to give up being in a cushioned environment to voice, safeguard, protect, and defend the rights of immigrants. Together, the two host the show, *The Rights of the Weak*, and as such they are appalled at hearing of the attack on Sarah.

While being courteous to Anisha, Adil is furious that she has chosen this moment to interview Sarah, who is still traumatized and most likely wants to be left alone. Amid their myriad arguments and general discussions about the racist treatment of various migrant communities, it is clear that Sarah still does not trust Anisha. Of course, she doesn't know that Anisha has quit the bureau on principle and as a matter of integrity. When Anisha suggests that Sarah is too liberal, she believes people too easily, and she too often insists on speaking to clients like Ahmad and finding out the truth for herself, Sarah is ambivalent.

Abel and Mary, who have seemingly appeared from thin air at this juncture, are inextricably linked to this story that is quickly emerging as a fight for justice over a great many wrongs. One wonders, though, whether at this point they realize that they might actually have to guide the players in this story and live up to their biblical connotations in real life. Even though the duo wishes to speak with Ahmad, Sarah is reluctant and not yet ready to share information about her client with people she scarcely knows. Sarah understands as a lawyer that protecting the confidentiality of her client is as much her duty as defending him. However, what finally dawns on her is that Anisha is also after the truth. Realizing this, she relents and agrees to discuss the matter with Ahmad to see if he is willing to speaking with Anisha or Abel and Mary.

Finally, the reporters and Anisha are ready to leave Sarah to what little remains of a rather eventful night. The two friends are glad once again that Sarah is safe and in good health. In a strange twist of fate, the incident appears to have united them and even prepared them to better fight the battle of truth together. At this point, Anisha hands a gun to Sarah and asks her to keep it, but Sarah refuses. As a believer in the law, Sarah firmly stands by her viewpoint that Ahmad will receive justice by means of a fair trial. Therefore, guns are not unnecessary here. Anisha, on the other hand, is the more cynical of the two, and her stint with the FBI has probably made her so. She does not really buy into Sarah's idealistic nature nor the trust that she places in people's inherent goodness.

Sarah walks into the SPLG office the next day as if nothing out of the ordinary has happened. She meets Ahmad, just as she would on any other day, to brief him on the upcoming master hearing that will take place in the coming weeks in San Francisco. The master hearing is the pleading part of the immigration proceedings in court. On this date the respondents (defendants) plead their cases and ask for a calendar date for the individual hearing where the merits of the case will be heard. Ahmad, on the other hand, is disturbed at the sight of Sarah's bruises from the previous night. When he asks her about them, Sarah casually brushes him off and says that racists had mugged her. She is angry about the whole incident, of course, and perhaps also worried, but she tries not to show this to Ahmad, who as a client is in need of nurturing. However, all of her efforts to retain her equanimity are suddenly shattered as she sees Anisha right outside of her office. It is not a welcome sight for Sarah, and she is angry at this intrusion into her client's privacy.

While Sarah is adamant that she does not want Ahmad speaking with anyone yet, Anisha is determined to find out whether Ahmad is a terrorist or not. Not surprisingly, both women appear to be on a quest for the truth, but they are going about it in their own separate ways. In the argument that follows, Ahmad surprises both by agreeing to speak with Anisha, saying that he has nothing to hide. Even though Sarah is not too pleased at the turn of events, she respects Ahmad's decision and lets him talk in detail about his past in the presence of Anisha. What he reveals is of course shocking and also sad, because it unravels the complete breakdown of the legal system and the faith that people place in law and order.

Ahmad's eyes are soft as his memory takes him back many years ago, when all of this began at an engineering college at a university in Iraq. Iraq, a proud country and the seat of the ancient Babylonian civilization, was at that time reeling under the rule of a tyrant, Saddam Hussein. The country had been transformed into a place where people were terrified to speak out against anything. No one knew what would happen if they spoke even remotely about the ruling government. Nobody knew how the country was being governed. Many people suffered under this repression, and many tales have come out of this phase, when people were treated worse than animals.

Ahmad remembers himself like any other student his age, as a young, idealistic person who was courageous and not afraid to speak his mind. One chance conversation that he had overheard probably changed his life forever. While walking around the college, Ahmad heard some students discussing Saddam Hussein and how he was an autocratic ruler.

The students' conversation was centered on revolution and hatred for the regime. Having overheard the conversation, Ahmad moved on with his own work. He was not aware of the repercussions that this might have on him. One night without warning, as Ahmad lay asleep in his house in Baghdad, a few men barged into his house and demanded to see him. Ahmad's hassled and worried mother didn't know how to react, and she was very upset, but no one paid any attention to her. With no explanation or notice, Ahmad was forcibly removed—practically dragged—punched, and taken away. He was cut off from the security of his family and kept in a completely unknown location.

Even in Ahmad's darkest nightmares, he had not imagined the torture that he would have to endure. He soon found himself in a small, dark, and dingy room surrounded by his tormentors. For some odd reason they seemed to think that he belonged with the CIA. They provided him with a vague and unknown reason, the government seemed to think that he was plotting against the regime and that he knew about American surveillance in Iraq. They kept asking him who he worked for and who his friends were. Ahmad was confused and utterly frightened at the immense hatred and cruelty that he experienced. He was treated like an animal, with men urinating on him. They were threatening to cut off his fingers one by one if he did not divulge the names of his friends. Ahmad, in his moment of despair told them that he would give them the names if they untied him. As part of the ploy, he tried to feign unconsciousness from weakness at being tied down. When his captors loosened his ropes and went out for a smoke, Ahmad saw his chance to escape. He ran into the darkness of the night, without even knowing where he was going or in which direction he was running. However, his freedom was short-lived, as he was soon caught again and taken to a different location. At this location a new group of men began torturing him all over again. Ahmad endured a life of unbelievable misery, fear, torture, and he had done nothing wrong. As a result of being arrested and tortured, Ahmad had lost his fiancée. Her family did not want her married to a man with a criminal record. As he comes back to the present as if in a daze and looks at Sarah and Anisha, his smile is ironic. This man, who was once accused of working for the CIA in Iraq, is now threatened and suspected by the very country for which he had been tortured in the first place. It is as if both the countries and their administrations are out to take revenge on a man, a peace-loving citizen, whose life has become a huge mess due to the political morass created by falsified intelligence reports on him. These reports have unjustly accused him of some of the most heinous crimes—crimes that he has not committed.

Nightmares

CHAPTER 2

ANISHA AND AHMAD

Sarah and Anisha cannot help but look helpless and saddened at what this man has had to endure. Still, Anisha is not totally won over in spite of hearing all of this. She wants to talk in more detail with Ahmad and find out more about him in order to be fully convinced. While Sarah and Anisha are still at loggerheads about why Ahmad needs to talk to Anisha, Ahmad is stoically philosophical about his predicament. He hopes that his religion will be better explained to the coming generations because Islam, does not propagate women being killed, or trees being cut, animals being killed, and churches being burned. Ahmad says, "the fanatics have made their religion appear as such to others". Ironically, he also does not harbor any animosity for his present agony, and he accepts it as just another phase of life that Allah perhaps had in store for him as a part of some bigger plan.

Anisha is still curious about what Ahmad stands for. To find out more about him, she takes him out for lunch. Amid talk and light banter, Anisha makes it very clear to Ahmad that she will not tolerate nonsense from him and that she will not hesitate to shoot him if necessary.

Anisha notices her attraction to Ahmad during the lunch. She likes the way he thinks, his honesty, his gentle style. Anisha, who is familiar with working with hardcore criminals, sees Ahmad as very different from the types of criminals she is used to and wonders if Ahmad will actually be able to stay in the United States.

It is time for Ahmad to face the immigration judge in a master calendar hearing, in which a date for the actual individual hearing and the pleading of the defendant or respondent is taken. The immigration court, like any other court, has one judge, but a jury isn't present and the set-up is quite informal. There isn't a person as court recorder, but there is a tape or digital recorder. In this particular case, a tape recorder is used. This is how it unfolds:

The court clerk sitting in the corner beside the judge calls for the case to begin.

Court Clerk: Case 015-564-092, Ahmad El-Jabbar

On one side sits the government attorney (the prosecutor) with a stack of files and his laptop. On the other side is Sarah, walking with her client to the table. The judge grabs the file from the court clerk, while smiling at her.

Judge [aside to the court clerk]: "I have my daughter's birthday tonight. I hope we can get things out fast."

Court Clerk: "I'll try my best, judge. You can't miss this one."

Judge [smiling at the court clerk]: "Yep. Can't miss it for anything in the world."

Sarah [looking at the judge]: "Good morning, Your Honor. Thank you for allowing me in your court today…And happy birthday to your daughter."

Judge: "Good morning, Mrs. Mustafagic. Thank you!"

Sarah: "It is an honor to be in your court."

She smiles and sits down, talking inaudibly to Ahmad.

Judge: "So, we are not on the record yet. What do we have here?"

Prosecutor: "I just got the file, Your Honor, so I have not reviewed it yet."

Judge: "I suggest the government reviews it."

Prosecutor: "Yes, Your Honor. It seems we have an arriving alien situation here."

Judge [looking at Sarah]: "Are you ready to plead today, Mrs. Mustafagic?"

Sarah: "Yes, Your Honor."

Judge: "Let's go on the record."

Judge [pressing the record button]: "This is Immigration Judge Trend on case number zero-one-five five-six-four oh-nine-two in San Francisco. Ahmad Al-Jabbar. Counsel, please state your appearances!"

Prosecutor [speaking in the microphone in front of him]: "Jeffrey Smith for the government."

Sarah: "Sarah Mustafagic for the respondent."

Judge: "Mrs. Mustafagic, you have indicated you are ready to plead."

Sarah: "Yes, Your Honor. We are."

Judge: "Go ahead."

Sarah: "We agree to the factual allegations one through four, but we deny number five in part."

Judge: "You mean, you deny number five?"

Sarah: "Yes, Your Honor."

Judge: "Do you concede removability?"

Sarah: "Yes, we do… And we decline to state a country of removal."

Judge: "The court will designate Iraq to be the country of removal, and I assume you are pleading for asylum?"

Sarah: "Yes, the reliefs requested are asylum, protection under the Convention Against Torture and Withholding, and alternatively, voluntary departure."

Prosecutor: "Your Honor, I do not think voluntary departure will be available in this case. Respondent is an arriving alien."

Judge: "Yes, I agree. You cannot get voluntary departure in this case."

Sarah: "So, no voluntary departure…But the other reliefs will be the same."

Prosecutor: "OK, Your Honor."

Judge: "Do you want to stop the clock on this or request an expedited trial?"

Sarah: "We would like to request an expedited hearing on this."

Judge [closing the recording device and checking his calendar]: "Let me stop the record and check on my calendar."

Immigration Court of San Francisco

Judge: "We can have the individual hearing on November thirteenth, 2005. Are the dates good for you, counsel?"

Prosecutor: "Yes, Your Honor. In the morning, right?"

Judge: "Yes, at nine a.m. in my court."

Sarah: "Yes, Your Honor, it's a good date."

Judge: "Let's go back on the record."

Judge [pressing the record button]: "Off the record, both parties have agreed to November thirteenth, 2005, at nine a.m."

Sarah: "Yes, Your Honor."

Prosecutor: "Yes, judge."

Judge: "I assume the language will be Arabic."

Sarah: "No, Your Honor, my client speaks perfect English."

Judge: "Are you sure?"

Sarah: "Yes, Your Honor."

Judge [smiling]: "English it is, then. Are you ready with your asylum application, or do you need more time, Mrs. Mustafagic?"

Sarah: "We are ready, Your Honor. May I approach the bench?"

Judge: "Yes, you may."

Sarah, giving a big package of paper to the prosecutor, walks up to the judge and hands him a copy of the same package.

Judge: "For the record, Mrs. Mustafagic has submitted asylum application with supporting documents. I will request the government to serve the respondent with the biographic information."

Prosecutor [handing a piece of paper to Sarah between the two desks]: "Please follow the instructions."

Sarah [smiling at the prosecutor, Jeffrey]: "We will."

Judge: "So, it seems we don't have to have another master hearing on this one. We'll move forward with the individual hearing. I really appreciate it when attorneys come prepared in my court. Thank you, Mrs. Mustafagic."

Sarah: "You are welcome, Your Honor."

Judge [looking at Sarah]: "Does your client waive the reading of the consequences of failure to appear? Have you explained to your client the consequences of failing to appear for the hearing?"

Sarah: "Yes, Your Honor, I have."

Judge [looking at the prosecutor]: "Anything to add?"

Prosecutor: "Nope."

Judge [looking at Sarah]: "Anything to add?"

Sarah: "Nothing, Your Honor. Except that my client is still wearing an ankle bracelet, and we will need to make sure we can finish this case soon."

Judge: "Yes, yes. I think the earliest time is November, anyway. If there's nothing else to add, the court adjourns."

Sarah: "Thank you, Your Honor."

Sarah walks up to the court clerk to pick up the notice and walks back, handing a copy to the prosecutor.

Sarah's tensions do not end with defending Ahmad in the court; she also has to manage media reports on him. Due to the sensitive nature of the case, the media is interested in reporting precisely what goes on in this case. No sooner has Sarah finished with the hearing and come out of the courtroom, Mary and Abel, radio reporters who report on racist activities, intercept her. While Abel and Mary are indignant about why they were not called in the event of such an important hearing, Sarah is more concerned about protecting the rights of her client, whom, she says, is being unfairly deported. She invites the reporters to be in court if they want to know more about what is happening in the case. When Mary and Abel ask Ahmad questions to learn more details from him, Sarah is annoyed at the intrusion into her client's life. She tells them that Ahmad's is a regular case and that they ought to leave him alone. However, Mary and Abel are not as easily deterred, and they probe further. Sarah is irritated and cautious, as she does not want the media to portray her client in a poor light, and she also does not want to give people the wrong idea about him, especially before the case has reached a conclusive point. As such, in spite of Mary and Abel's well-intentioned attempts to learn more about Ahmad, Sarah is very clear that she cannot allow either Ahmad or the reporters to discuss the case and have several facets of this intricate case be falsely reported. Thus far, Sarah is not really aware of the crucial role that Abel and Mary might play in the story, and so she remains tight-lipped about the entire case and her interpretation of what Ahmad is going through.

Ahmad Coming to the US

As Mary and Abel are racking their brains in their endeavor to find out more about Ahmad, Anisha meets with people who are apparently colleagues working on the same project as her. She is nevertheless reminded of her job and the necessity to act on behalf of Ahmad. At times like this, one is truly confused about Anisha. What exactly is she up to, and what is her goal in knowing Ahmad? It seems rather intriguing that Ahmad is keen to meet her, though he is also curious and somewhat hesitant. In fact, Ahmad and Anisha appear to have embarked on a strange association in which neither can fully trust nor mistrust the other, and yet there is a growing urge to learn more about each other.

Ahmad's hesitation about how he should go about meeting Anisha increases greatly after an episode at Anisha's house. Ahmad is unable to go out much due to his anklet restrictions, he decides to meet Anisha at her home to answer her questions. However, what starts out as an innocuous question-and-answer session takes an unforeseen turn when Ahmad sees Anisha not very discreetly changing her clothes as he is hovering around. Ahmad is aroused at the sight of Anisha's silhouette, which is discernible through her thin clothing. All of a sudden, Anisha tries to kiss him. This is all very unexpected for Ahmad, who is unprepared and unaccustomed to such behavior. Anisha, however, does not make a big deal out of the issue, and after Ahmad expresses his surprise and reluctance, she apologizes and moves away. However, unlike Anisha, who might have dismissed the entire episode, and for whom it might not be a big deal to kiss a man, Ahmad keeps mulling it over, recalling it often. Ahmad is of course not your average American; his upbringing is far more traditional, and this is unorthodox behavior for him—something that has unsettled his mind. The cultural differences between Anisha and Ahmad are hardly insignificant, yet the tangential ways in which their relationship develops are charming: from anger on Anisha's part to curiosity to an attraction of sorts. Ahmad is obsessed with the entire episode with Anisha, but he does not know what to do next. Like a child seeking guidance, he confides in Sarah when he meets her to prepare for the case. He confesses that he likes Anisha, which totally shocks Sarah because she did not see this coming. Sarah is visibly agitated, expressing her displeasure, as she thinks that Anisha is up to no good and is out to lure her client into revealing to her something that he ought not to. There is considerable bad blood apparent between Sarah and Anisha at this stage, and in spite of the two being friends, their mutual trust has borne the brunt of it. As a lawyer, Sarah is mindful that her client's interests need to be safeguarded at all costs, and she instructs Ahmad to not meet Anisha again, as she believes it could have ramifications on the case hearing that they are preparing for.

In the meantime, Mary and Abel are still pursuing every avenue to obtain as much information as they can about Ahmad. Asking Ahmad's brother, Muhammad, would be the obvious thing to do, but they want an outside opinion on this. Their search takes them through different people, and they finally find a restaurant owner who has known Ahmad and his family. Mary meets Shawn Singh, a restaurant owner who has been friends with Ahmad's brother. A successful Punjabi businessman, Shawn tries to help whomever he can. He still remembers his roots, and in spite of having been a victim of racism many times, he tries to contribute to society by employing as many people as he possibly can.

CHAPTER 3

VIOLENCE SPILLS OVER

During a lull in the day, when the restaurant is empty, Mary decides to interview Shawn. However, like so many others in the US, she is oblivious to the difference between someone from Iraq and someone from India—or, for that matter, the difference between a Muslim and a Sikh. To her, all of these people are categorized as non-white people, which is likely synonymous with non-American people. In spite of Shawn rather naïvely telling her that he is from India, Mary asks if he has come from Iraq too, like Ahmad. In many ways, this is perhaps the root of several misunderstandings in different minds in the US, who tend to group everyone who is not Caucasian into the same category. When Mary presses Shawn on the question of whether Ahmad could be a terrorist, Shawn laughs and totally dismisses the accusation, adding that he has known the family for a very long time, and he doesn't believe any of them to be terrorists, even remotely. As they are talking, three men wielding baseball bats enter the restaurant. Just then, Abel walks into the restaurant and looks suspiciously at the men. When Shawn tells them that the place is closed and will reopen in two hours, the men jeer at him. Sensing trouble, Abel tries to stop Shawn from approaching the men. But it is already too late. Suddenly, one of the men, Harry, hits Shawn on the head before Abel can stop or warn him. Utter chaos ensues in the restaurant. As Abel tries to protect Shawn, another man, known as Francis, holds him back. During the uproar, Mary tries to call 911, but before she can speak into the phone, it is snatched away from her hand, and the third man, George, pushes her against the wall and hits her across the face. Mary grabs a bottle of chili sauce and presses it into George's eyes, which makes him let out a scream. Harry starts swinging the bat and striking Shawn. It is complete mayhem. Harry is repeatedly screaming, "You Muslims, killing our people." Francis hits Abel again and again. Everyone is crying and hysterically screaming in pain. At that very moment, the sound of sirens pierces the air, and the attackers stop their attack, ostensibly frightened for the first time. Cursing the cops and Muslims in tandem, Francis spits on Abel and calls the duo good-for-nothing Jews as Mary hysterically shouts that Shawn is not a Muslim but a Sikh—words that are apparently wasted on the attackers.

Attack

The preponderance of gun culture in America has led to the killing of Sikhs in various places in gurdwaras (Sikh temples) or in restaurants. Such crimes are branded as some of the most heinous racist murders in history. For the first time, Abel and Mary have to face the fact that sometimes the American youth are extremely ignorant about other cultures and religions, perceiving everyone with turbans and beards as fundamentalists. The tendency to generalize and lump everyone into the same category in the wake of 9/11 is perhaps an extremely paranoid, xenophobic reaction on the part of certain individuals that only breeds more bigotry. Hate propaganda is also systematically permeating American culture. Shawn, while convulsing with pain, screams what many people fear: "If the greatest nations of the world behave like this, what does the future look like?"

The bullies flee, leaving behind a wrecked shop, a hysterical Mary, and a battered Abel and Shawn. They also rip off Mary's shirt and take it with them. Mary, Abel, and Shawn crawl across the shop floor, too shocked to react to what has just happened to them.

Abel and Shawn have been hospitalized due to the injuries they have sustained. Mary is extremely worried, and she doesn't know what she should do next. She calls Sarah and informs her about the incident. A worried Sarah immediately decides to go down to the restaurant to survey the scene, and she takes Ahmad with her. Meanwhile, when Mary speaks with the doctor about Shawn and Abel at the hospital, she is told that while they are all right, Abel needs a blood transfusion. The hospital does not have his type of blood, but as luck would have it, Sarah and Ahmad, who are already there, ask what type of blood Abel needs, and Ahmad points out that since he has O postive blood, it can be given to anyone. It is ironic that those surrounding and affected by Ahmad's ongoing case are also saved by his blood. Once the formalities and blood transfusion procedure are over, Abel is reported as being in stable condition, and everyone breathes a sigh of relief—especially Mary, Sarah, and Ahmad. In between expressing her relief that Abel is fine, Mary is convinced that the attackers need to be found. Ahmad suggests that perhaps Anisha, being an FBI agent, can help. Needless to say, this suggestion does not play well with Sarah, and even though she keeps it to herself, her face betrays her feelings. Mary, of course, has no idea about the underlying tension that has manifested itself between Anisha and Sarah, and she takes the opportunity to suggest to Sarah that in the wake of all of this trouble, it would be good if Sarah could support Abel and Mary in building their story and finding the truth behind Ahmad's case.

Sarah Talking to a Colleague

Meanwhile, one would question what is behind Anisha's actual interest in this case. She is in regular touch with someone who has an opinion on Ahmad and who wants her to work on some kind of case. One cannot help but wonder what Anisha is up to and what her real intentions are and whether Sarah's fears about Anisha are not misplaced. But Anisha, too, is no longer the FBI agent who was very sure of what the FBI had told her. Somehow, Anisha's faith in authority appears to have been shaken, and she begins to question many other things as well. Perhaps she is no longer certain about Ahmad's role as a terrorist, and one wonders if she is actually close to sympathizing with him because of her own feelings for him or whether she truly believes that a grave injustice has been committed against him. Anisha is tremendously confused and angry as she yearns to follow her heart and instincts.

It is soon time for Ahmad to appear in court again, and he and Sarah are anxious about how the proceedings will go. The proceedings then begin in the Immigration Court, San Francisco, for the individual hearing.

Judge: "Are we ready to proceed? Should I go on record?"

Prosecutor: "Your Honor, I have a request before we continue."

Judge: "Hmm. Go ahead."

Prosecutor: "We would request the respondent's counsel to give us the originals of the important documents provided for a forensic—"

Sarah: "Sure. Do you have any particular document in mind?"

Prosecutor: "Hmm. At this point, the government does not believe in the authenticity of the birth certificate and the letters of recommendations provided."

Judge: "Hold on, hold on—I think this should be on the record."

The judge presses the recorder.

Prosecutor: "OK."

Judge: "This is Judge Trend on the matter of Ahmad El-Jabbar. Counsels, please state your appearances."

Sarah: "Sarah Mustafagic for the respondent."

Prosecutor: "Jeffrey Smith for the government."

Judge: "Off the record, the government has indicated that they want to get certain documents for forensic authentication. The respondent has agreed."

Sarah: "Yes, Your Honor, we can go ahead and provide such documents."

Judge: "OK. Let's proceed with aligning the exhibits of the case."

Prosecutor: "Sure."

Sarah: "Yes, Your Honor, let's do that."

Judge: "Exhibit One. Application form I-five-eight-nine for an application of asylum, withholding and Convention Against Torture. Exhibit Two..."

Mary, meanwhile, is back where she belongs: the radio station. She thinks that listeners should be informed that Abel is in the hospital and therefore cannot come on the show with her. This is in itself an adequately derogatory statement that might help listeners understand how an average person's life can be disrupted by the hate being spewed by people like those who had attacked them. She decides to talk on their radio show about Abel and how they were attacked. She also reveals that he is in the hospital as a result of such fanaticism. Mary tells her listeners that the worst part is that the person who was targeted, Shawn, is not even a Muslim, stressing that these fanatics are not using their common sense or understanding to judge a person. She reinforces the basic tenet that even if Shawn were a Muslim, it will still be wrong for them to attack him. Assumptions made by people who have no idea about what they are doing can be dangerous. Through her radio show, Mary has brought up some pertinent points and raised awareness among her listeners, but whether she can make an impact or even change a few minds remains to be seen.

As the lines are opened for callers to voice their opinions on the issue, the first call is another hate call from someone named Frank.

Frank: "Hmm…Hello, am I on air?"

Mary: "Yes, you are."

Frank: "First, of all, you liberals are all the same—"

Mary: "What do you mean?"

Frank: "Our country is under attack, and you bunch of bitches keep talking about protecting the Muslims, Jews, Mexicans, and whatever—we are at war!"

Mary [in a high tone]: "War against who, Frank?"

Frank: "Against all of them…And you traitors are helping them."

Mary: "There is no them against us, Frank. There is only humanity and justice."

Frank: "No! There is only America…The rest does not count! If it was me, I would beat the shit out of all you…and bang you bitches and then hang you all for punishment."

Frank hangs up.

Frank's profane language on the air is often typical of misunderstandings on the war on terrorism. He accuses Mary of being a terrorist supporter, and he goes on to threaten her with death or rape because she sides with people who, according to him, are neither Americans nor friends of America. Though deeply disturbed by the call and the ominous threats, Mary gathers her strength and tells the caller about the true American and how being an intolerant fanatic is not helping the cause of the peace-loving citizens of the country. Thankfully, people like Frank remain a minority, and very soon other callers who support Mary in her endeavors call to tell her that they welcome such initiatives.

CHAPTER 4

A SUCCESSFUL COURT CASE

The case continues in immigration court.

Judge: "Did you submit your witness list, counsel?"

Sarah: "Yes, we did, Your Honor. Unfortunately, one of our witnesses withdrew."

Prosecutor: "I would like to point out to the court that this is prejudicial to the case."

Judge: "Well, I will decide on this."

Sarah: "We will still be presenting two experts and one person to testify for Mr. Al-Jabbar."

Prosecutor: "Your Honor, we reserve the right to bring more witnesses."

Sarah: "Objection, Your Honor. We should be advised in advance about who is going to witness."

Prosecutor: "Your Honor, we will not disclose our witness list yet."

Judge: "Hmm. I will request the government to disclose the list at least thirty days prior to the continuation of the trial."

Sarah: "I agree, Your Honor."

Prosecutor: "We firmly object."

Judge: "Noted and overruled."

Sarah: "Thank you, Your Honor."

Judge: "Seems we need to call it a day. We will schedule another session in two weeks."

Prosecutor: "The government requests a continuance until forensic is done on the originals. We agree to keep the clock running."

Judge: "Any objection, Mrs. Mustafagic?"

Sarah: "How much time are we talking about?"

Prosecutor: "I don't know, Your Honor. Around ninety days."

Sarah: "We agree, as long as the clock keeps running—allowing Mr. Ahmad to obtain his work permit."

In court proceedings, if the "clock is waived," it requires the court to give priority to the case to be processed instead of being scheduled years from the master calendar hearing. Unfortunately the immigration courts are quite overwhelmed, and they still delay on such cases. If more than one hundred and fifty days have passed, not by the fault of the asylum applicant, the government has to issue a work permit. This allows the applicant to obtain work and even obtain a driver's license and other benefits. During that time, if the clock is waived, none of these benefits will follow unless the case is completed and won.

Judge: "So be it. We are adjourning, and the date we can reconvene will be January fifteenth, 2006. Anything to add?"

Sarah: "No, Your Honor."

Prosecutor: "Nothing else."

Judge: "The court adjourns."

After the court session adjourns, Sarah and Ahmad decide to have lunch together. Relaxed, they casually discuss the case and the efforts of the government lawyer. Just then, out of the blue Anisha appears, surprising both Ahmad and Sarah. Sarah displays her annoyance at Anisha's presence, and when Anisha asks to talk to Ahmad, Sarah however, interrupts and tells her that she wishes to speak with Anisha privately. As soon as Sarah and Anisha are alone, Sarah asks Anisha what her intentions are with Ahmad. She is not sure what Anisha is up to, and she doesn't want any kind of trouble for Ahmad. Sarah at this point confronts Anisha, accusing her of playing with Ahmad's feelings. Sarah knows well that Ahmad is not used to such behavior and that Anisha can use her gender to entice Ahmad to give confidential information. Sarah tells Anisha that unless she stops her games, she will ultimately ask Ahmad to obtain a restraining order against her. Since Anisha is not acting in the capacity of an FBI agent, this should not be difficult. Anisha, perhaps for the first time, is caught off guard and confesses to having kissed Ahmad, but she dismisses it as just an impulse of the moment.

Sarah is shocked at the revelation and visibly angry with Anisha. She clearly does not want Anisha to be associated with her client in any way, and she thinks that Anisha is bad news for Ahmad. Perhaps she is even more worried because Ahmad himself has revealed that he likes Anisha. Anisha tries to justify what happened between her and Ahmad by emphasizing that as an adult, Ahmad is free to decide what or whom he likes or dislikes. She then throws the ball into Sarah's court, asking her whether her dislike in seeing her and Ahmad together stems from the fact that Sarah herself has started liking him. This is an accusation that Sarah, of course, vehemently denies. And yet, Sarah makes it quite clear to Anisha that if she meddles with her client or his life in any way that is harmful to him, she will be answerable to Sarah. Anisha, for her part, tries to reassure Sarah that her interest in Ahmad was merely a fleeting moment of weakness. She wanted to kiss him, but she is unsure whether she has any feelings of affection for him. On that note, the two women part ways feeling animosity all over again. Anisha heads out on her own, while Sarah joins Ahmad to resume their conversation about the case.

Sarah Talking to Anisha

In the meantime, Abel is well enough to leave the hospital. Mary drives him back home, where Sarah and Ahmad are waiting to welcome him. Ahmad thanks Abel for his generosity in defending him, telling him that he is a very courageous man—a compliment that Abel takes with a grain of salt, as he is not too certain that he is pleased to have been involved in the whole fiasco in the first place. Amid the jubilation and happy homecoming, however, Abel realizes that Shawn has been released too, and Ahmad's anklets have been removed. There is something inexplicable that illness does to people, bringing unlikely individuals close together. Through this episode, Abel and Mary appear to have become closer to each other, discovering an intimacy that they had never known before. After Sarah and Ahmad have left, Mary drives Abel home. They are left to themselves to explore their feelings for each other with greater depth.

In another setting, another couple seems to be discovering their feelings for each other. When Anisha calls up Ahmad to invite him over for dinner, she asks him if it is true that he likes her. When Ahmad confirms that he is attracted to her, Anisha is happy, and the two agree to meet at her home. They are also celebrating the fact that Ahmad has now received a work permit and his driver's license. As a result, he feels that life's little joys really ought to be celebrated. Ahmad is not too sure how Anisha feels about his affection for her, and she too is taking it as it comes. Soon, though, when they reach her house and are in an intimate setting by themselves, Ahmad and Anisha both discover that their affection for each other is full-blown and deep. The way in which two people come together in the most unlikely of circumstances is indeed serendipitous.

It is also strange how one good deed begets another: Abel finds this out in the dentist's office. Apparently, word gets around, and the dentist whom Abel has come to see is a Sikh who has heard of Abel supporting and helping Shawn, who is a Sikh as well. He thanks Abel for supporting the community. In gratitude, he offers Abel preferential treatment over other patients, who are typically catered to on a priority basis. Not surprisingly, though, Abel is uncertain of his involvement in the case or the developments thus far. One can almost sense his cynicism and detachment from it all, even as the doctor's goodwill is proof of this reciprocity. Like in the Bible, Abel's life of obedience to righteousness costs him his life. Here, Abel sacrificed himself to protect another and almost died.

They say that there are myriad things around the world that conspire to bring truth, love, and happiness together, and this would seem to be the case with Ahmad. In what turns out to be a very important development in this instance, Mary receives a phone call from one of her contacts from the Middle East telling her that Ahmad has never been connected with terrorism in any way and that all of the charges against him are fabricated. Mary's contact, Terry, adds that the CIA has given Ahmad a clean clearance as well, and it should now be abundantly clear to everyone that he has simply been a hapless underdog in an unfortunate imbroglio with no small amount of bad luck to exacerbate his predicament. Abel and Mary are both relieved that the man they have been so closely associated with has been vindicated. It now seems that all of the pain that they went through for Ahmad was well worth it.

January 15, 2006, at the immigration court in San Francisco.

Judge Trend is presiding. The trial commenced two hours earlier. Ahmad is in the witness box, testifying, and Sarah is conducting a direct examination.

Sarah: "How many times have you been tortured?"

Ahmad: "Three times."

Judge: "Was it at the same location?"

Ahmad: "I do not remember, judge. It was hurting too much."

Prosecutor: "I don't understand."

Judge: "Let me play the record back."

Prosecutor: "OK, I get it."

Sarah: "At this point, I would like to call our first witness, Dr. Salima George."

Judge: "Dr. Salima George, let me put you under oath. Do you swear to tell the truth, the whole truth, and nothing but the truth, so help you God?"

Dr. Salima: "I do, Your Honor."

Judge: "Have a seat on the witness stand."

Sarah [addressing the doctor]: "So, tell us about your background."

Dr. George: "I have a PhD in psychology, specializing in victims of torture, and I was born in the Middle East, so I understand what is happening there."

Prosecutor: "Your Honor, we object to this witness for lacking sufficient foundation to be accepted as an expert."

Judge: "Overruled."

Sarah: "Your Honor, Dr. Salima George will testify how Mr. Al-Jabbar shows the traits of someone who has been tortured."

Prosecutor [argumentatively]: "Are you an Arab, or what?"

Sarah [outraged]: "Objection! Your Honor! This is argumentative."

Dr. George: "I don't know if I should be offended. I'm a US citizen, and I swore allegiance to this country."

Judge: "Mr. Smith, what is your point? Objection sustained. May I see you both in my chambers?"

The judge takes them to his chambers.

In the judge's chambers with Sarah, and prosecutor Smith:

Judge: "I am very unhappy with you, Mr. Jeffrey Smith. This is no way to behave in my court."

Prosecutor: "But, Your Honor—"

Sarah: "I was offended too."

Prosecutor: "I apologize to the court."

Judge: "One more such comment, and I will have you excluded, do you understand?"

Prosecutor [embarrassed]: "Yes, judge."

They all walk back into the immigration court ten minutes later and return to their respective seats.

Judge: "Let's go back on the record and resume the examination of Dr. Salima George."

Sarah: "Tell us your findings on Mr. Al-Jabbar."

Dr. George testifies of the condition of Ahmad, stating that he showed signs of torture. After one hour of questioning, Sarah continues.

Sarah: "Doctor, you were saying that he suffers from PTSD, post-traumatic stress disorder?"

Dr. George: "Yes, he does. All of the symptoms are consistent with his behavior."

Sarah: "Doctor, in your experience, why would you say..."

The examination continues for hours, as they discuss the different aspects of the asylum.

Judge: "We'll be adjourning soon. Let us reconvene in two weeks."

Prosecutor: "No objection, Your Honor."

Sarah: "So, should we should say two weeks? In two weeks I will be out of town."

Judge: "Let's say in a month. Is the fingerprinting current? And it seems the biometrics were done properly, right?"

Prosecutor: "Yes, Your Honor."

Judge: "Adjourn."

CHAPTER 5

THE AMERICAN SENSE OF JUSTICE PREVAILS

Special Agent Anisha

It appears that good fortune is finally smiling upon Ahmad, as he has begun to believe in his freedom and well-being again. The mystery surrounding Anisha and her clandestine meetings with Dan are also about to unravel. During her own investigation on Ahmad's case, Sarah has called some of her contacts. During a discussion, someone says that Anisha has often operated undercover, but it is almost impossible to confirm. Sarah, not willing to take the chance, picks the phone up and tells Anisha that she wants to meet her. Anisha agrees, and the two meet at Anisha's house. Sarah reaches Anisha's house and rings the bell. Anisha opens the door, and without saying anything, Sarah walks in looking furious.

Anisha [looking at Sarah]: "Hi. Salaam."

Sarah: "Salaam."

Anisha: "Are you still pissed at me or what?"

Sarah [in a rude tone]: "Pissed is an understatement, you leech, bitch, cheap woman—"

Anisha: "Hey, hey...You are my guest, so cool down."

Sarah: "There's nothing to cool down. You are a disgrace. You took advantage of an innocent man, pretending to love him, and all this time you have been undercover. Are you not ashamed?"

Anisha: "What are you talking about?"

Sarah [looking at Anisha in the eye]: "You didn't leave the bureau, and I know when you are lying to me."

Anisha: "What is your problem? Even if I didn't leave, it is my job, and who the hell are you to tell me what to do?"

Sarah: "So it is true and confirmed: you are undercover. And who do you report to? NSA, CIA, FBI?"

Anisha: "So you don't have any clue. You are just trying. Right?"

Sarah: "Who cares? I know you just like I know myself, and I know I am right."

Anisha: "Hmm...Well, who cares now. Yes, I have been undercover."

Anisha had been working as an undercover agent for the FBI all along, without ever having left the bureau, contrary to what everyone had been led to believe, and her mission had been to discover everything about Ahmad—something that she hopes will not make Ahmad angry with her. It is, of course, a happy coincidence that she fell in love with Ahmad. And when Dan confirms to her that Ahmad is innocent, she is deliriously happy and decides to come clean—at least in front of Ahmad. Anisha is a brave woman and an honest one at that. She has no desire to start her life with a man she loves on the basis of a lie. So on that day, when Ahmad comes home to her, she has been praying, and she pulls off her scarf from her head, as if she is divulging all of her secrets for him to see. She tells him how she was working with the agency all along. She also shares that while she might have lied about being an agent, her feelings for him are not a lie. At this moment, Ahmad, in spite of being in much trouble, graciously forgives Anisha for her faults. Ahmad readily accepts Anisha and tells her that he loves her very much. Anisha and Ahmad, despite being forward thinking, do not wish to break the traditions of their religion and get physically close before getting married. Now that Ahmad's case looks positive, they want to get married and seek the blessings of their respective parents prior to settling down in holy matrimony.

Anisha, with Her Islamic Scarf, Praying

In the meantime, Sarah is very happy with the way things are going. She has also assumed importance as a lawyer because of her dedication to her work and her panache with solving critical issues. The Ahmad case has finally taken on a positive tone, among a few other cases that she has won. Her dedication has earned her the trust of her clients and also much-needed respect from the society and community in which she works. As a result, Sarah is invited to the radio station to speak with people about immigration issues. Sarah readily agrees to talk to people on radio because she believes in spreading the message of justice. Once she is on the show, in addition to being a lawyer, Sarah's genuine concern for the people and their concerns comes through. As always, though, certain nasty people continue to criticize whatever one does. One of the callers on the live show questions her loyalty to the country, since she is seemingly working to save people who might be terrorists. But Sarah is clear about her mission; she believes that she owes her allegiance only to the United States of America, its people, and the legal system under which she has taken an oath to protect the interests of the country and those who are innocent. Her talk show on the radio show is inspiring and informative. While she discusses how the Patriot Act and the Real ID Act have not helped immigrants, she also advises those who cannot afford a lawyer about how they should approach NGOs who work in the field of immigration.

The life of the immigrant who has been charged on suspicious grounds and those who are in direct contact with the immigrant never seem to be short on excitement. During yet another hearing in Ahmad's case, while the prosecutor and Sarah are busy presenting their own cases, the judge is summoned by an emergency. He is informed that his wife, Palestinian woman, has been attacked. Alarmed, he hurries home to find his wife traumatized. The FBI agents at his residence have been given jurisdiction, since this a federal case. The judge is startled to learn that there may be a pattern in the attacks that have victimized Sarah, Shawn, Abel, and now his wife. According to the FBI agents, Anisha, and her colleagues who are investigating the case, the probability that the same culprits are behind the case is high. Anisha, however, opts out of the investigation because it concerns a person she is closely associated with.

There was, of course, never any doubt about Anisha and Ahmad liking each other, but now that they have fallen in love, they can't seem to live without one another. The most important thing for their parents is their happiness, Anisha and Ahmad soon get approval from their parents, and the wedding day arrives. Who would have thought that two people who could not even see eye-to-eye would end up getting married? The wedding follows Muslim tradition. An imam (Muslim priest) attends, along with Sarah, Abel, Mary, and the guests. It is a small wedding at this point because Ahmad's case is still running, and the couple hopes that once Ahmad's case clears immigration that a huge party will follow.

Anisha and Ahmad Falling in Love

When Ahmad meets Sarah next, it is as a married man and in the presence of his wife, Anisha. As a lawyer, Sarah is delighted because the marriage means that Ahmad no longer needs to go for an asylum petition, as his wife is a US citizen. However, Ahmad is stubborn in this matter. He points out that since he was tortured, he wants to seek asylum. Even though Anisha has her reservations about this, Sarah understands well what her client is going through, and she explains to Anisha why it is important for Ahmad, to seek asylum as a person. Sarah, however is worried about losing a witness, which could be prejudicial. Anisha is determined to not let her husband be deported, and she tells Sarah that she wants to petition for him. Like any experienced lawyer, Sarah advises them that they should think it over and decide what they want to do before making the final call.

While everyone is concerned about the attack on Judge Trend's wife, what is more worrisome is the connection between those who attacked Sarah, Shawn, and Judge Trend's wife. Mary and Abel decide to find the attackers, but there is something brewing that makes everyone unsure of the circumstances.

One evening as Anisha and Ahmad are walking in the sunset, discussing their plans for the future, they are accosted by three men; the very same men who had previously assaulted Sarah and Shawn. They are armed with baseball bats and knives. Anisha and Ahmad are totally unprepared for such a situation, and they are taken aback. They are at a complete loss as to how to respond. It seems that the men are determined to kill Ahmad, who, they believe is the root cause of all of the trouble. They start hitting Ahmad with baseball bats, while pulling Anisha by her hair. Suddenly, as if out of nowhere, Shawn comes to their rescue and hits one of the men, Harry, with a shovel. In the thick of the ensuing melee, as Shawn and Harry are striking one another, Anisha takes the opportunity to draw her gun. She does so while dialing 911, announcing herself as an FBI agent. She cleverly then arrests the men at gunpoint; she demands to know what they want from Ahmad. The men admit that they think Ahmad is a terrorist, and they want to rid the country of terrorists and anyone who supports them or associates with them. They also confess that this was the reason they attacked Sarah and Judge Trend's wife.

The police soon arrive, and the men are taken away in handcuffs. Anisha then thanks Shawn for his timely intrusion, which actually saved their lives. Shawn and Anisha also discover, to their mutual delight, that they are both from Punjabi decent, a brave sect of people known for their courage and valor. However, like everyone, they too are apprehensive about the situation. Anisha promises to be in touch with Shawn once Ahmad has recovered from the incident. The vicious attack on Ahmad affects everyone around him, making them all wary. When Sarah comes to see Ahmad and Anisha, she voices her concern too. Sarah comforts Anisha, who is still reeling from the thought that Ahmad could have actually been killed; telling her that having the police record of the attack could enable Ahmad to file for a U visa, which would be less of an ordeal than going through a trial for asylum. U visas are for immigrants who are victims of certain crimes. Sarah, as always, assumes the role of a counselor for her client. She advises Anisha that instead of petitioning for him, as Anisha had planned, applying for a U visa would be a far better choice, particularly as Ahmad's male ego is likely to make him reluctant to accept his wife Anisha's help. Sarah also explains to Anisha that it's also possible that the marriage could be construed as a fraud, since it took place during Ahmad's proposed deportation period. In spite of the fact that Sarah, as their lawyer, knows that their marriage is authentic, she believes that it is better to avoid such complications. Sarah further advises that even though obtaining a U visa would mean that Ahmad might have to wait for three years before actually getting his green card, it is certainly more preferable than applying for asylum. Anisha agrees to speak with Ahmad once he has recovered and is able to think more clearly than he can in his present condition.

When a case such as Ahmad's surfaces, there are many elements of the story to piece together. Sarah has an unexpected visit from Shawn, who after the Ahmad case is scared that the police now have information on him in their records. He is frightened that he might be deported. Shawn tells Sarah that he had come to the US on a visitor visa but did not return. Instead, he remained and established a restaurant. He narrates how he had been attacked earlier in connection with the same case. He also reveals that he has spoken with the district attorney on the case, who was both sympathetic and helpful, but Shawn is now worried because of his police records, even if it is for a good cause. Sarah, nevertheless, advises Shawn that his good deed of helping Ahmad might actually work to his advantage, since he can now apply for a U visa as a victim of a hate crime with felonious assault. Shawn could get a work permit with a U Visa, and his family could stay for three years, within which he could apply for a green card. To Shawn, who is at his wit's end, Sarah appears to be an angel. Indeed, for many people who have been frustrated by immigration complications that restrict their lives and make them live in fear forever, she is an angel.

Suddenly, a lot of things look different. Instead of asylum, Ahmad plans to change his plea to "Adjustment of status through marriage." Accordingly, Sarah, Ahmad, and Anisha present themselves in the court of law.

Sarah shows up in immigration court with Ahmad a few months later.

Sarah: "Your Honor, at this point in time, we would like to ask for a continuance and amend our plea to adjustment of status through marriage."

Judge: "What?"

Prosecutor: "Hold on! Hold on! Who is marrying whom?"

Sarah: "Mr. Al-Jabbar is now the spouse of a US citizen."

Judge: "Congratulations, Mr. Al-Jabbar, and who is the lucky winner?"

Anisha [sitting in court]: "Me, Your Honor."

Judge: "You, Agent Anisha Adath? Oops…Now I need to think. Do I have a conflict here?"

Prosecutor: "I do not see a conflict, Your Honor."

Sarah: "Well, Your Honor, we would like to withdraw the asylum and request the court to wait for the adjudication of the form I-One-Thirty, relative petition, and the form I-Four-Eight-Five, adjustment of status."

Judge: "Adjustment of status? I think this part is with me, Mrs. Mustafagic."

The immigration marriage petition process requires a two-part documentation. One is the form I-130 (marriage to an immediate relative), and the second part is the permanent residence, which is the adjustment of status to obtain a permanent residence. This is also known as the form I-485 petition. If someone is not in deportation, these two parts are usually filed with the United States Citizenship and Immigration Services (USCIS). However, if the person is in deportation, then the action is divided in parts. Part one is filed with the USCIS, and part two is filed with the immigration court. This is the reason the judge mentions he has to adjudicate an adjustment of status, which usually occurs when someone is in deportation or removal proceedings. However, there is an exception when it comes to "arriving aliens," which is a category of people entering the United States. In this case, Ahmad is considered an arriving alien.

Prosecutor: "I will assume the same, judge."

Sarah: "No, Your Honor. Al-Jabbar is an arriving alien. Therefore, the jurisdiction lies with the USCIS."

Judge [checking his manual]: "Hmm. You are right."

Prosecutor: "Well, Your Honor, we will object to the situation of having the asylum plea to be withdrawn by the respondent."

Judge: "Well, Mr. Smith, he is withdrawing before a decision, and there is no indication it was a frivolous asylum. So, I will grant the withdrawal."

Prosecutor: "Well, for the record, we will want to enter our objection."

Judge: "Noted. So, I assume you will either want to terminate the proceedings or leave it with the court until the case is granted by USCIS or denied."

Sarah: "We will keep it until it is finished."

Judge: "So, should we put this off for another six months?"

Sarah: "That works for me."

Prosecutor: "OK with me, judge."

Judge: "Adjourned until the next case. And, Mrs. Mustafagic, I might have to recuse myself from this case."

Sarah: "OK, Your Honor."

The process has to be validated at the USCIS office, where both Ahmad and Anisha have to undergo interviews in order to determine that their marriage is bona fide. Anisha and Ahmad are advised of the consequences of lying. They both undergo rigorous interviews, and after checking and rechecking all relevant documents to ascertain their authenticity, they finally emerge victorious. Their marriage is approved, and they are thrilled. In some ways, it has been a test of their connection to one another and of the trying times, which are finally coming to an end.

It has been several months since Anisha and Ahmad met Sarah, and it is now time for them to appear in court again. Understandably, after all that has occurred, Ahmad is tense, but Anisha is now by his side to soothe his nerves. Sarah then calls them to her office.

Sarah [with a serious face]: "Well, I have news for you!"

Anisha: "Stop making faces. Tell it to us straight. We are ready to face this together."

Sarah [smiling]: "As usual, Anisha, you are always ready for the worst."

Ahmad: "Tell me, Sarah, what is next."

Sarah: "Well, I have great news. Ahmad does not have to be in court anymore, as Judge Trend has just granted Ahmad's motion to terminate, meaning the court case is closed. Ahmad now has a green card and is a free man!

Anisha: "Are you kidding?"

Sarah: "No, I am not. His green card will be mailed in the next three weeks."

Ahmad cannot hold his joy and starts crying and thanking Allah that he has been accepted in this country. Ahmad can barely believe his ears. For Ahmad and Anisha, this is great news, and they are deeply grateful to Sarah for all that she has done for them. In fact, she has been nothing less than their guardian angel. Amid it all, Ahmad, ever the pious man, does not forget to thank God, nor the fact that he had promised to feed the poor if ever he were released peacefully as a permanent resident.

Everyone loves good news, and Ahmad's situation has touched considerably more people than his immediate family. Everyone involved has come to partake of the celebrations. At the radio station, Abel and Mary are ecstatic upon hearing the news of Ahmad's release. They are even more excited because the members of the racist, vigilante gang have been arrested and sentenced to no less than forty-five years in prison for committing hate crimes. The station celebrates the victory of American justice over matters of injustice toward innocent people. They also make special mention of Sarah, who has done an incredible job of believing in her client and defending him. Shawn calls the radio station to thank Sarah for her contribution to his case, which has also resulted in jubilation for the entire community. There is special recognition for those who had stepped forward to help Ahmad in his fight for justice. Ultimately, though, it is a victory for the people and their faith in the American judicial system.

Reflecting on Ahmad's Case

CHAPTER 6

TIME TO REJOICE

The victory is a cause for a celebration. Ahmad and Anisha's union was highly intriguing. This relationship brought an end to Ahmad's nightmare, and it also brought him happiness.

At the party, everybody is dancing to Indian and Arabic music, including Judge Trend, who was also invited. Mary and Abel are also present. Sarah [to Abel]: "Hey. How are you?"

Abel: "Doing well. So, what's new?"

Sarah: "Well, we just got a call. The government just shut down an entire school in California, around two thousand students. They're after the students for visa violations."

Abel: "Hmm."

Sarah: "Do you know what's ironic about this case?"

Mary [joining the conversation]: "What?"

Sarah: "It seems that all of the students were just victims of a scam. Instead of working with them, the government just went after them."

Abel: "Here we go again. Give us more details."

Sarah: "Give me a few days. For now, let's just enjoy ourselves."

Interested, Mary chats with Abel and tries to get more details from Sarah. But Sarah is not interested in talking about immigration at this point. Sarah looks at Abel and Mary. Sarah [smiling]: "Chill out. I just want to enjoy myself. It has been a long fight."

ABOUT THE AUTHOR

Born in a small village on the beautiful tropical island of Mauritius, Shah Peerally moved to the United States in the 1990s, where he studied law. After graduating, he formed the Law Offices of Shah Peerally, which ultimately became the Shah Peerally Law Group PC.

During his law school days, Shah was a witness to the sad events of 9/11, which naturally   caused wide spread anger. Consequently, Shah noticed a lot of indiscriminate violence on the immigrant community in the US. As an immigrant and a law student, it was difficult for him to understand the motivation behind the religious extremism being rampantly practiced.

His main concern then as it is now, is to save the immigrant community from unnecessary backlash and branding as terrorists. It was with this thought that he helped create the "Know Your Rights" guide for immigrants, which went on to become extremely popular, because it spoke as a voice for many immigrants. He later followed up with various speeches in different churches, temples and mosques teaching immigrants about their civil rights and how they should learn to fight back.

Today, Shah Peerally is an attorney licensed in California, practicing immigration law. The Peerally Law Group deals with issues related to the United States Citizenship and Immigration Services (USCIS), Immigration and Custom Enforcement (ICE) and Customs Border Patrol (CBP) under the Department of Homeland Security (DHS).

Shah's work has assumed meaningful proportions, especially with the assistance he provided to the students of Tri Valley University, during the scam that affected so many students from outside. As a lawyer, Shah has also acted as a face for many while petitioning the U.S. Government to change laws related to immigration that discriminate against innocent immigrants.

As a part of his work in spreading the message of rights for immigrants and creating awareness, Shah has graduated to film-making under his home banner, Shah Peerally Productions Inc.. As a part of this, he has scripted the film *Shattered Freedom* which was selected at the Third World Movie Festival. In addition he is the executive producer of various sensitive films that deal with immigration issues, such as *The Lost Dream*, *The Immigration Fraud*, *The Immigration Interview* and also *H4 The Curse*. The films and his book are an attempt to highlight important problems with regards to immigration and the plight of immigrants.

www.ingramcontent.com/pod-product-compliance
Lightning Source LLC
Chambersburg PA
CBHW071346130626
46556CB00005B/2055